To
the lovely children
in Reception class
of H.W Cofe school

Best wishes

R. H. Broth

CW00865594

RB Dedicated to my Mum and Dad,
who always believed in me and encouraged
me to pursue my dream.

I hope you enjoy my first book!

JB For Sam & Alice

VANESSA STARTS PRESCHOOL

Written by R.A. Booth
Illustrated by Jake Biggin

Her name is Vanessa,
three years of age.
She lives with her Mum, Dad
and her rescue dog, Paige.

It's the first day of preschool.
Vanessa is looking glum.
She really doesn't want to go.
"I want to stay home with Mum!"

When Mummy drops her off,
Vanessa begins to cry.
Her teacher, Miss Leach
urges her to say, "Goodbye!"

With so many new faces around her,
Vanessa doesn't feel better.

But when Miss Leach shows
her round, a smile replaces
the frown.

Vanessa has made a friend.
Isabelle is her name.

They are playing at the sand pit.
Their happy giggles sound the same.

It's lunchtime now,
Vanessa is glad to hear.
She tucks into her fish pie,
grinning from ear to ear!

"Who's tired? It's nap time!"
calls Miss Leach.
"Come and lie down on the mats,
and have a little sleep."

Vanessa isn't very tired,
so she's allowed to go and play.

There are so many exciting things to do.
"Please can I play with this clay?"

Painting colourful pictures of unicorns,
making model dinosaurs from play dough.
Playing fun games outside in the Wendy house,
and being very creative with Duplo.

It's nearly time to go home.
Vanessa's mum has arrived.
Miss Leach collects her paintings.
Vanessa hopes that they have all dried.

"May I come back tomorrow?"
Vanessa asks her mum.
"Yes, of course you may," she smiles.
"Looks like you had lots of fun!"

The end

Printed in Great Britain
by Amazon

82069425R00016